For Pekka, Olivia, Julia and Doris the wiry-haired dachshund, my carbon busting family   LC

We select our printing facilities with care. This book was printed in the USA using soy-based inks. The paper includes 10% post consumer waste (PCW) recycled content. The paper is Forest Stewardship Council (FSC), Sustainable Forest Initiative (SFI), and Programme for the Endorsement of Forest Certification (PEFC) certified. The book parts meet or exceed all CPSIA guidelines for Pthalate Lead content.

The Singing Dolphin

Requests for permission to make copies of any part of the work should be submitted online at info@mascotbooks.com or mailed to Mascot Books, 560 Herndon Parkway #120, Herndon, VA 20170

PRT1111A

Printed in the United States.

ISBN-13: 978-1-936319-95-4
ISBN-10: 1-936319-95-0

www.mascotbooks.com

A Carbon Busters™ Eco-Adventure

The Singing Dolphin

Laurel Colless

Meet the Carbon Busters

Hi! We're Wanda, Chu, Peter and Riva. We became the Carbon Busters on the day we met. Four baby trees had been left to die in the empty lot near where we live. We worked hard together clearing the trash, pulling the weeds, and watering the dirt. We didn't let those trees die.

Earth Diva watched us from her sofa in the sky and awarded us her highest honor. That same day, Earth Diva also introduced us to her unusual family members. Do you want to meet them too?

There's the Shooster, who spins us through the air and magically changes the empty lot into a secret place, just for us. We call it Our Meadow and it's where all our Carbon Busters adventures begin. Sometimes we get there and Earth Diva is out of balance. Other times, when there's too much carbon in the air, Captain T (for temperature) has bad fever. And Doctor Flower and his dog Doris need our help when Poco, the mini-flying saucer, measures pollution trouble.

When it's time to leave for an adventure, the Shooster spins around our four trees -- the redwood, the birch, the elm, and the oak -- and changes them into super scooters. They're called Pulitos. They can fly, swim, or ski anywhere using only nature's energy. They take us to some really surprising places: under the sea, over the desert, and even inside plants and animals. Sometimes we get help along the way from Doctor Flower's science teacher, Senorita Sinta. And if we really get stuck, we call the voice of Invisible Bu-h. That's Earth Diva's sky uncle, who tells us 'knock-knock' jokes and always knows what to do.

We're pretty sure there's going to be an adventure today. We can feel it. You can come with us if you like. But don't forget the Shooster!

SHOOSTER

RIVA

PETER

WANDA

CHU

Earth Diva

Captain T

Doris

Senorita Sinta

Dr Flower

"THE SEA...

is where I would like to be." Peter told Riva, Wanda, and Chu. "I would stay in the cool water all day and all night – and maybe even all the next day."

The Carbon Busters were at the park but it was too hot to play.

"Ouch." cried Chu. "Double ouch!" He jumped off the burning slide.

"I forgot to tell you it was too hot for sliding," Riva giggled.

"A bit late now," mumbled Chu, his head lowered.

"Are you okay, Chu?" Wanda asked faintly. "It's so hot. Even a little breeze would be nice."

Almost as she spoke, Wanda felt her long blond hair rise up slightly at the ends.

"Shooster, is that you?" Wanda sat up straight, searching the sky around her. "It is you!" she said. The Shooster swirled into view, blowing a cool breeze onto all four kids and lifting a large red plastic bag from the top of an overflowing trash can behind them.

The Carbon Busters all jumped together to try to catch the bag, but it blew just out of reach and flew off, bobbing and swooping, down the street. "Oh no! We have to catch it," Peter shouted. "It would be very bad if a plastic bag were to go in the nature."

"Hurry," cried Chu, "it's moving towards the empty lot."

5

The Carbon Busters forgot about being hot as they chased the red plastic bag towards the four trees at the empty lot. Peter finally managed to catch the plastic bag in midair, just as the Shooster spun them all magically through the trees to the other side.

Flying through the air, they watched the redwood, the birch, the oak, and the elm shoot upwards. Hills popped out where their houses had been and instead of the road, clean water ran through a cool stream. One after another, the Shooster dropped them gently onto new green grass.

"Our Meadow!" said Peter, folding the plastic bag and putting it into the deep pocket of his just-too-big jacket. "This is nature as it really could be."

"Nice catch, Peter," said Dr. Flower, who stepped out from behind the redwood tree, followed closely by Doris the dachshund. "Kids, I'm glad you're here. Poco just flew in to report a bad situation." Dr. Flower held out Poco, his silver saucer-shaped plant and animal happiness meter. He gave the voice control command, "Poco- Reading!"

The Carbon Busters watched as Poco beeped and spun around on the palm of Dr. Flower's hand. Doris began barking loudly, and a red cloudy image rose above Poco's metal dome top.

r. Flower's eyes narrowed. "Minus 2...and it's an animal...very serious."

Wanda's voice was sorrowful. "What kind of animal? Where?"

Dr. Flower stowed Poco hastily in his belt pocket and said, "I'm not completely sure Wanda, but Doris and I will come with you as far as the sea."

"The sea?" exclaimed Peter. "Yes!"

At that moment, the Shooster blew up around them, almost lifting them off the ground.

"Here we go!" Riva said with a smile.

"Don't forget the Shooster!" They all shouted together, laughing as they tried to follow the Shooster's darting green eyes.

Suddenly, the four trees began to wave in the wind. The kids knew what that meant. The Shooster plunged into the center of the meadow and pushed them off, running as fast as they could towards the trees: Wanda to the birch, Chu to the oak, Riva to the elm, and Peter to the redwood.

Squealing and laughing, they circled the trees as the Shooster Spin chased them round and round; faster and faster, turning each tree into a super Pulito scooter -- one for each Carbon Buster. Peter's green helmet was flashing.

"Peter, it looks like you're the leader," said Riva. "And look, we're all wearing funny rubbery clothes."

"Wetsuits," said Chu nervously.

When they arrived at the edge of the cool blue sea, Doris, who was not fond of water, jumped off Peter's Pulito before he even had time to stop.

Dr. Flower stepped down after her. "You can take it from here," he said, shaking Peter's hand.

"Thanks," said Peter, looking out at the breaking waves and wondering what lay ahead.

"Let's go!" called Wanda from the back of the line. Peter hesitated a moment, then pushed his Sazoo joystick forward, plunging slowly into the shallow waves. He wobbled a little as his Pulito wheels automatically folded under and converted into surf skis. The others followed quickly behind him.

"Wow!" said Chu.

"Whee!" said Riva.

"Whoaaa!" said Wanda, who got bumped into the water by a wave.

"Are you okay?" called Peter.

"Sure," said Wanda, spitting salt water out of her mouth. "I just wanted to test the water temperature," she said. "It's nice." The others laughed and waited for her to climb back on her Pulito. Then they pushed through the gentle waves together and rode out to the open sea.

After they had been traveling for a while, Riva thought she heard a strange high singing sound. She looked out to the horizon and wondered if it might be a mermaid.

"Can you guys hear that?" she asked the others.

"I can't hear anything," called Peter, "but I sure can smell something. It's awful." Soon everyone else smelled it too.

"Peee-ew!" said Chu. "What is it?"

"It's trash - everywhere," said Wanda looking around sadly. The Pulitos were slowing down as they pushed through bobbing plastic bottles, plastic cartons, and old plastic bags with rotten stuff inside them.

"Is that a diaper?" Riva pointed as it floated past.

"Fish don't wear diapers. Double Peee-ew," said Chu.

"I just wonder where all this trash came from?" said Riva. "Maybe it got dropped off a boat or came from somewhere on the beach?

"Maybe," said Peter, thoughtfully. "But it would take a lot of boats and a lot of beaches to produce this much trash."

"Guys, I know where it came from," Wanda said. "This is what happens to trash when someone drops it in the streets. It goes down into the drains, and then into a river, and finally it goes out to sea."

"Oh," said Riva, "but why do people have to drop litter in the first place when we have trash cans?"

"I guess people don't imagine their garbage would travel this far," Wanda replied, looking around sorrowfully.

"And end up poisoning the sea," added Chu.

Riva said, "Well anyway, we're going to take all these bottles and cans back to our recycling bin, right, Peter?"

Peter looked around hopelessly at the island of trash, "Ah, it's probably too much for us to carry. Also, shouldn't we really be getting on with finding the unhappy animal?"

"Let's see what's in the prop box. That might tell us what we have to do next." Chu suggested.

"Good idea, Chu," Peter said as he climbed around to the front of his leader Pulito and lifted the lid.

"What's in there?" asked Wanda, driving up next to him.

"I'm...not...quite sure." Peter said, leaning in curiously.

He pulled out an enormous green see-through bag with two ropes attached to it. The words GARBAGE LASSO were stamped on one side of it. Peter held it up to the others. "Look, everyone! I think it's some kind of enormous trash bag."

"Come on! Let's try it," urged Riva.

Peter hesitated and then swung the rope around his head like a cowboy lasso. "Yee haw!" he cried, tossing it far out in front of him. The lasso bag landed neatly over one of the largest clumps of floating trash.

"Hooray!" the others cheered.

"Everyone, let's start rounding up the rest of the trash inside the floating lasso," Riva commanded. She charged forward, accidentally creating a large wave that splashed right over Chu.

"Hey! Watch out," Chu growled. He leaned over to steady himself and right at that instant, his hand touched something slippery in the water. Chu froze with fear.

"Hey, look! Is that a dolphin?" squealed Wanda, pointing into the water. "I knew I heard something."

"I think it's a dolphin," called Peter excitedly. "And there's another one!"

Chu laughed, mostly with relief.

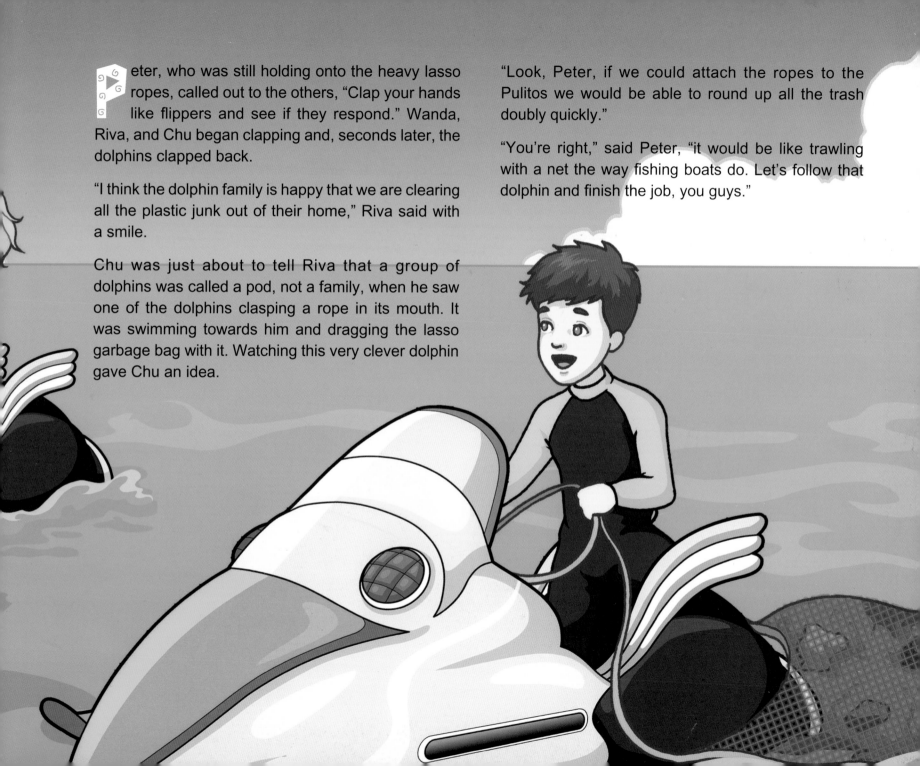

Peter, who was still holding onto the heavy lasso ropes, called out to the others, "Clap your hands like flippers and see if they respond." Wanda, Riva, and Chu began clapping and, seconds later, the dolphins clapped back.

"I think the dolphin family is happy that we are clearing all the plastic junk out of their home," Riva said with a smile.

Chu was just about to tell Riva that a group of dolphins was called a pod, not a family, when he saw one of the dolphins clasping a rope in its mouth. It was swimming towards him and dragging the lasso garbage bag with it. Watching this very clever dolphin gave Chu an idea.

"Look, Peter, if we could attach the ropes to the Pulitos we would be able to round up all the trash doubly quickly."

"You're right," said Peter, "it would be like trawling with a net the way fishing boats do. Let's follow that dolphin and finish the job, you guys."

Once they got started, they were able to fill the large net very quickly. Some of the dolphins came behind them and helped by zigzagging up and down, rounding up any stray pieces of trash. One of the dolphins even became skilled at flipping plastic bottles through the air and landing them right in the net.

"Goal!" cried Peter, clapping when the dolphin managed to toss a large half gallon jug from a long distance right into the opening of the net.

"Hooray!" The others shouted, and the dolphin squealed loudly in reply.

Trawling for trash was fun, and they had almost finished when a sweet little dolphin that seemed smaller than the rest poked its head up from the water and started to sing. It was the same high-pitched song that Riva had heard earlier.

"So lovely," said Wanda adoringly.

"It must be saying thank you to us for cleaning up its home," Riva said happily.

Unfortunately, the little dolphin interrupted its song with small coughing noises. Peter suggested that maybe it had a cold, but then the dolphin stopped singing altogether and began making scary high-pitched wheezy sounds, as if it was trying to breathe but couldn't.

"Quick! That little dolphin is sinking." Peter jumped into the water and tried to hold it up, but the dolphin began thrashing around unhappily and it was too slippery for Peter to support. Wanda and Riva splashed into the sea beside him, but they couldn't get a grip on the dolphin either. Chu didn't want to say it, but he wondered fearfully if the Singing Dolphin might have eaten plastic trash.

The dolphin continued to cough and wheeze. It became clear to the kids that it must have caught some of the plastic trash in its throat.

"Let's quickly call Dr. Flower," said Peter, clambering up out of the water and back onto his Pulito. He pressed DF on his dashboard and when Dr. Flower's image appeared, Peter hurriedly reported that they had found the animal with the minus 2 happiness level – it was a little dolphin that was having trouble breathing.

Dr. Flower fell silent for a few moments. "You'll have to go in, Peter," he said finally.

"Go in? Uh, where?" asked Peter, looking over at the others and then at the dolphin. "Do you mean go into the dolphin?"

"That's right," Dr. Flower nodded.

"But how?"

"Don't forget the Shooster," Dr. Flower called out firmly.

Before there was time for further discussion, the Shooster blew in forcefully, throwing Peter into a high-speed spin. It looked at first as if the Shooster had made Peter disappear, but then the others realized that Peter had actually been shrunk. The voice of Little Peter came out as a very cute squeak. The other three watched anxiously as Little Peter tried to drive through a small water ripple, which to him must have looked like a rising wave on a high sea.

"Peter's no bigger than a pea," observed Chu with amazement.

Dr. Flower's image on the Pulito dashboard was also now so small, they could hardly see him. Riva, Wanda, and Chu bent down as close as they could to hear the conversation.

"Are you ready to go in now, Peter?" asked Dr. Flower.

"Yes," he squeaked, nervously. "I'm going to hurry inside before another diaper comes by." The others laughed loudly, their mouths wide. The gasping dolphin, who was watching them, opened its mouth as well. Just at that moment, the Shooster lifted Peter and blew him straight down the surprised dolphin's throat.

sing the light of his Pulito's headlamps, Peter was able to continue the steep, downward journey into dolphin's throat. He had lost his connection to Dr. Flower but he wasn't worried, as it would have been too noisy to talk over the sound of the dolphin's raspy breath.

Peter was also getting tossed around a lot by the irregular air currents. In fact, he had to put all his concentration into staying upright and following the navigation map on his Pulito screen. He checked his map and saw that he was heading towards a red flashing target "X" at the base of the Singing Dolphin's throat.

Peter's Pulito stopped automatically when he reached the target. He wasn't sure what to do next, so he shone his headlamps all around the space. Immediately, Peter noticed a piece of thick plastic that was blocking one part of the dolphin's throat passage. No wonder the Singing Dolphin can't breathe, thought Peter. Without hesitating, he reached up and gave the plastic a hard yank. It didn't budge. He tried again, using all his strength, this time managing to free the plastic.

"Task completed. Yes!" Peter said aloud as he wadded the plastic up and put it in his pocket. "Now all I have to do is get out of there."

Peter turned the Pulito around and began driving back towards the Singing Dolphin's mouth. He couldn't wait to tell the others what had happened. But when he was almost back to the mouth area, his headlights began to dim. The word EMPTY flashed on his screen and then...silence.

Peter let out a loud sigh as he sat in darkness, wondering what to do. His Pulito was out of energy and the dolphin's mouth remained firmly closed.

utside on the sea, the others were getting worried. The little dolphin was resting on the water and seemed to be breathing more calmly now, but where was Peter?

"Where could he be? What's taking so long? He must be in danger." Wanda worried.

"I have a good idea," said Riva. "I'm going to try to make the dolphin sing again. You guys get as close to the dolphin as you can," she instructed, "and when it opens its mouth, you peep inside and look for Little Peter."

Riva stood up on her Pulito and began to sing a beautiful made-up song. Almost immediately, the little dolphin opened its mouth to sing with her.

"They're doing a duet," Chu laughed.

"And it's working!" Wanda slipped into the water and swam towards the dolphin's mouth.

"Look! Here comes P-Peter!" laughed Chu, pointing at the pea-sized Peter as he slid through the air, gliding along on the sound waves of the dolphin's tune before settling back onto the sea.

Everybody clapped, including the dolphin, then the Shooster spun Peter straight back to his regular size.

"What a ride!" exclaimed Peter. He dove into the water and swam over to hug the Singing Dolphin. "I hope you're feeling better now, my friend." The dolphin squealed and then swam happy circles around Peter. He giggled, especially when the dolphin began to nibble playfully on Peter's ear.

"My ears are very ticklish," Peter laughed.

"No fair!" laughed Riva, jumping in. They both joined Wanda and Peter in the sea, and everyone enjoyed swimming with all the dolphins in the clean, trash-free water.

Soon the sun began to go down, so they started preparing to head back to shore. The Shooster waved goodbye to them and sped away.

"The Shooster has worked hard today. He's probably going home to unwind," said Riva, laughing loudly at her own joke.

It was only then that Peter remembered that his Pulito energy cell was on empty. "Oh no! I should have asked the Shooster to charge my batteries with some wind power," said Peter.

The sea was completely calm and the sun was almost gone.

"What other clean energy choice do you have?" asked Wanda worriedly.

The Singing Dolphin, who had been observing Peter's dismay, suddenly released a very loud whistle from its newly cleaned throat. This was followed by the speedy return of a number of dolphins, swimming and leaping through the water at great speed.

Then without warning, the Singing Dolphin swooped underneath Peter and raised him up above the water on its back.

"This feels like clean energy that could also be fuuu-n," squealed Peter.

"Dolphin energy!" they all shouted together as they watched Peter, arms clasped tightly around the dolphin's neck, whooshing towards them.

"Last one to the beach is a wet diaper!" called Peter, laughing as he flew past them towards the distant shore.

When they finally got to dry land, Dr. Flower and Doris were there to greet them. Doris was looking forward to licking someone's salty toes and ran straight over to Chu, who giggled and squirmed. Then, after they had shouted a final goodbye to the dolphins, Dr. Flower began hauling up the trash. Peter rolled onto the sand. "I think that was the bravest I've ever had to be on an adventure," he said with a long tired sigh. "Now, I'm exhausted."

"Well, you did tell us that you wanted to be in the sea," said Wanda, kneeling down on the sand next to him.

"I did," Peter said, "but I would just like you all to know that just for today, I have now had enough of

 ...The Sea"